THE AMAZING ADVENTURES OF THE DC SUPER-PETS!

The Blue Tiger Burglars

by Steve Korté

illustrated by Mike Kunkel

Based on characters created by
Bob Kane with Bill Finger

PICTURE WINDOW BOOKS
a capstone imprint

Published by Picture Window Books, an imprint of Capstone.
1710 Roe Crest Drive
North Mankato, Minnesota 56003
capstonepub.com

Library of Congress Cataloging-in-Publication Data
Names: Korté, Steven, author. | Kunkel, Mike, 1969– illustrator. | Kane, Bob,
creator. | Finger, Bill, 1914–1974, creator.
Title: The blue tiger burglars / by Steve Korté ; illustrated by Mike Kunkel.
Description: North Mankato, Minnesota : Picture Window Books, [2022] |
Series: The amazing adventures of the DC super-pets | "Based on characters
created by Bob Kane with Bill Finger." | Audience: Ages 5–7. | Audience:
Grades K–1. | Summary: When the Penguin and his gang steal a rare blue
tiger cub from the Gotham City Zoo it is up to Batgirl and Misty, her crime-
fighting Super-Pet, to catch the thieves and return the tiger.
Identifiers: LCCN 2021054290 (print) | LCCN 2021054291 (ebook) |
ISBN 9781666344257 (hardcover) | ISBN 9781666344295 (paperback) |
ISBN 9781666344301 (pdf)
Subjects: LCSH: Batgirl (Fictitious character)—Juvenile fiction. |
Superheroes—Juvenile fiction. | Supervillains—Juvenile fiction. | Cats—
Juvenile fiction. | Tiger—Juvenile fiction. | Theft—Juvenile fiction. | CYAC:
Superheroes—Fiction. | Supervillains—Fiction. | Cats—Fiction. | Tiger—
Fiction. | Stealing—Fiction. | LCGFT: Picture books.
Classification: LCC PZ7.K8385 Bn 2022 (print) | LCC PZ7.K8385 (ebook) |
DDC [E]—dc23
LC record available at https://lccn.loc.gov/2021054290
LC ebook record available at https://lccn.loc.gov/2021054291

Designed by Kay Fraser
Design Elements by Shutterstock/SilverCircle

TABLE OF CONTENTS

She is a fearless feline.

She has night vision
and powerful paws.

She is Batgirl's loyal companion.

These are . . .

THE AMAZING ADVENTURES OF

Misty the Crime-Fighting Cat

CHAPTER 1

Trouble at the Zoo

Deep inside the Batcave, Batgirl is working at the Batcomputer. She is reading the latest news stories. Sleeping beside her is Misty, her crime-fighting feline friend.

"A blue tiger cub is arriving at the Gotham City Zoo tonight," says Batgirl. "It's one of the world's rarest tigers."

Batgirl turns to Misty. "I'm worried that Catwoman might try to steal the tiger and add it to her rare cat collection," she says. "I'm going to stand guard at the zoo. Misty, will you keep an eye on the Batcomputer?"

Misty yawns and nods her head.

Batgirl jumps on the Batcycle and

zooms out of the Batcave. Misty

hops onto a chair and stares at the

Batcomputer.

Later that night, the blue tiger cub arrives at the zoo's nursery. Batgirl stands guard at the door to the room.

Suddenly, the lights go out, and the entire room falls dark. When the lights go on again, the tiger is gone!

"That's odd," Batgirl says to herself.
"I was standing at the door, and no
one went past me."

Batgirl then looks up and sees a
skylight in the ceiling. It is wide open!
Someone must have grabbed the tiger
and pulled it up through the skylight.

CHAPTER 2

The Fowl Felons

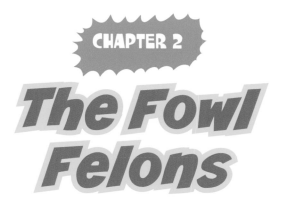

Batgirl runs outside and looks up in the air. Two birds are flying above her. One of the birds is Artie Puffin, and the other is Griff the vulture. They are carrying the tiger cub in a net.

"Catwoman didn't steal the tiger," says Batgirl. "The Bad News Birds are behind this crime. Those fowl felons work for the Penguin!"

Batgirl jumps on the Batcycle and chases the birds.

Suddenly, the birds fly over the edge of a steep cliff. Batgirl can't follow them. She calls Misty on the Batphone.

"The Bad News Birds have stolen the blue tiger," she says. "I need your help!"

Misty looks around the Batcave and
sees the Batcopter parked in a corner.
She gulps nervously and then hops into
the aircraft.

Misty reaches her paw and pushes
the "start" button.

WHOOOOSH!

The vehicle soars into the air and

flies out of the Batcave.

CHAPTER 3

Misty to the Rescue

Misty steers the Batcopter toward

Artie and Griff. The two birds are flying

toward a grassy field. The Penguin

waits there for them.

"Be careful with that tiger, boys!"

calls out the Penguin. "Catwoman will

pay me a fortune for that feline!"

Misty pushes a button on the

Batcopter control panel.

ZIP!

A large net shoots out of the vehicle.

It wraps around the two birds and the

tiger cub.

The Penguin frowns and points his umbrella toward the Batcopter. A thick stream of green slime blasts out of his umbrella.

Before the slime reaches the Batcopter, Misty tips the vehicle sideways. The helicopter's swirling blades now point directly toward the Penguin.

The high winds created by the

spinning blades blow the slime back

toward the villain. The sticky goo covers

him completely.

"ACK!" squawks the Penguin.

Misty flies back to the cliff, where Batgirl is waiting.

Misty lowers the net holding the two villainous birds and the tiger. Batgirl pulls the tiger from the net and ties up the birds with her Batrope.

Batgirl and Misty return the blue tiger to the zoo and lock Artie and Griff in a cage. As a zookeeper cares for the rare cat, Batgirl picks up Misty and cradles her.

"Nice job, Misty," says Batgirl. "As always, you are a *purr-fect* crime fighter!"

Misty snuggles into Batgirl's arms and purrs with happiness.

AUTHOR!

Steve Korté is the author of many books for children and young adults. He worked at DC Comics for many years, editing more than 600 books about Superman, Batman, Wonder Woman, and the other heroes and villains in the DC Universe. He lives in New York City with his husband, Bill, and their super-cat, Duke.

ILLUSTRATOR!

Mike Kunkel wanted to be a cartoonist ever since he was a little kid. He has worked on numerous projects in animation and books, including many years spent drawing cartoon stories about creatures and super heroes such as the Smurfs and Shazam. He has won the Annie Award for Best Character Design in an Animated Television Production and is the creator of the two-time Eisner Award-winning comic book series Herobear and the Kid. Mike lives in southern California, and he spends most of his extra time drawing cartoons filled with puns, trying to learn new magic tricks, and playing games with his family.

"Word Power"

feline (FEE-line)—any animal of the cat family

felon (FELL-uhn)—a criminal convicted of severe crimes

fortune (FOR-chuhn)—a large amount of money

fowl (FOUL)—a bird, such as a chicken, turkey, or duck

nursery (NUR-sur-ee)—a place for the care of young animals

rare (RAIR)—not often seen, found, or happening

skylight (SKYE-lite)—a window in a roof or ceiling

steer (STEER)—to move something in a certain direction

villain (VIL-uhn)—a wicked, evil, or bad person who is often a character in a story

villainous (VIL-uhn-uhs)—relating to wicked or criminal behavior

WRITING PROMPTS

1. Batgirl and Misty use the Batcave as their secret hideout. Write a paragraph about a hidden hideout of your own. Then draw a picture of it.

2. The blue tiger cub is very rare. Write a short story that explains where it came from and how it got to the Gotham City Zoo.

3. What happens to the Penguin and his birds at the end of the story? Write a new chapter that explains how the villain helps them escape from the zoo.

DISCUSSION QUESTIONS

1. Batgirl thinks Catwoman will steal the blue tiger cub from the Gotham City Zoo. Why does she think that?

2. Why does the Penguin need Artie Puffin and Griff the vulture to carry out his plan? What can they do that he can't do by himself?

3. If you could have a crime-fighting pet, what would it be? What kind of powers or special skills would your Super-Pet have?

THE AMAZING ADVENTURES OF THE DC SUPER-PETS!

Collect them all!